Written by Gaby Goldsack
Illustrated by Steve Smallman

This edition published by Parragon in 2010

Parragon
Queen Street House
4 Queen Street
Bath BA1 1HE, UK

Printed in China
All rights reserved

ISBN 978-1-4454-0611-4

Worried Hen

Illustrated by Steve Smallman

ParRagon

Bath · New York · Singapore · Hong Kong · Cologne · Delhi · Melbourne

It was an icy cold day and Farmer Fred had just finished milking the cows.

"Shivering onions, it's freezing," he said to Patch his sheepdog, as he toasted his toes in front of the fire.

Suddenly, the door swung open and Farmer Fred's wife, Jenny, burst in.

"Hetty Hen has hatched twelve beautiful chicks," panted Jenny. "Now there's just one egg left to hatch."

"Woof! Woof!" barked Patch.

As Farmer Fred pulled on his wellies, Patch ran over to the hen-house to check on Hetty Hen's progress.

There were twelve fluffy new chicks huddling together. Hetty Hen was still keeping the thirteenth egg warm.

"What's happening?" Patch asked
the other animals, who had gathered
round to watch.

"Sssshhh!" whispered Connie Cow.
"Hetty's concentrating."

Hetty waited and waited. And the
other animals waited and waited.
But nothing happened.

"It's just too cold in this hen-house," clucked Hetty Hen. "This egg is never going to hatch."

"Here, cover the egg in some of my feathers," said Dotty Duck. "They always keep me lovely and warm."

"Have some of my wool," said Shirley Sheep. "I think you'll find it very cosy indeed."

"And take some of my hay," said Connie Cow. "It will warm up that egg in no time."

Hetty Hen covered the thirteenth egg with the feathers, wool and hay. Then she sat on top. She was just getting comfortable when Farmer Fred arrived singing a song.

"Happy Hatch Day,
dear Hetty,
happy Hatch Day
to you!"

When he had
finished, Farmer Fred
sat down beside
Hetty and waited.
Farmer Fred waited
and waited. Hetty
waited and waited.
And the other
animals waited and
waited. But nothing
happened.

"It's just too cold in this hen-house," said Farmer Fred. "But never fear, I've an idea!" he cried. Then he disappeared into his workshop.

Before long, lots of banging and crashing could be heard.

The animals all looked at each other and shook their heads. What was Farmer Fred making this time?

A few minutes later the door to the workshop swung open and out stepped Farmer Fred. He was carrying a see-through box in his arms.

"This," he declared grandly, "is a Super-heated Egg-hatcher. All we need to do is pop the egg inside and it will hatch before you can say *Eggstraordinary!*"

"In you go," said Farmer Fred. He popped the egg into the Super-heated Egg-hatcher.

Then everybody sat back and waited. Farmer Fred waited and waited. Hetty waited and waited. All the animals waited and waited. But nothing happened.

Nothing happened, that is, until there was a pop and a fizz and the lightbulb flickered out.

"Never fear!" said Farmer Fred. "It just needs a new lightbulb." And off he went to the farmhouse.

The animals gathered outside the hen-house.

"We've got to help poor Hetty," said Dotty Duck. "Surely someone must have an idea." She looked at each animal in turn. But they just shook their heads.

"Woof! Woof!" barked Patch, wagging his tail. He had just remembered where the warmest place on the farm was.

Woof!
Woof!

Farmer Fred was sitting beside the fire sorting through a box, when Patch burst through the door.

"Hello Patch," smiled Farmer Fred, as he popped a lightbulb into his cap. "This is no time for lazing around the warm fire. We've got an egg to hatch."

"Woof! Woof!" barked Patch, as he picked up the cap and placed it gently beside the fire.

The animals gathered outside the hen-house.

"We've got to help poor Hetty," said Dotty Duck. "Surely someone must have an idea." She looked at each animal in turn. But they just shook their heads.

"Woof! Woof!" barked Patch, wagging his tail. He had just remembered where the warmest place on the farm was.

Woof!
Woof!

Farmer Fred was sitting beside the fire sorting through a box, when Patch burst through the door.

"Hello Patch," smiled Farmer Fred, as he popped a lightbulb into his cap. "This is no time for lazing around the warm fire. We've got an egg to hatch."

"Woof! Woof!" barked Patch, as he picked up the cap and placed it gently beside the fire.

Farmer Fred looked at the bulb inside
his cap beside the fire.

"That's it! I've got a brilliant idea," he
cried, grabbing his hat and rushing out
of the farmhouse.

Farmer Fred dashed outside and came back with the unhatched egg in his cap. Hetty Hen and her twelve little chicks followed him into the warm kitchen.

"There," said Farmer Fred, laying the cap and egg beside the fire.

Everyone sat back and waited. Farmer Fred waited and waited. Hetty waited and waited. And the other animals waited and waited.

"Oh, dear! Oh, deary me!" clucked Hetty Hen. "This egg is never going to hatch!"

But, just then, CRACK! The egg began to hatch…and out popped the thirteenth chick.

"Cheep! Cheep!" chirped the chick, hopping onto Farmer Fred's lap.

"It looks like she's decided you're her mum, Fred," laughed Jenny, as she walked through the door.

"I always knew this was the warmest place on the farm for hatching eggs," smiled Farmer Fred.

"Woof, woof!" barked Patch.